SOMETHING LOST
SOMETHING FOUND

By Natalia Paruzel-Gibson
Illustrated by Laura Catrinella

Natalia Paruzel-Gibson

◆ FriesenPress

Suite 300 - 990 Fort St
Victoria, BC, V8V 3K2
Canada

www.friesenpress.com

ISBN
978-1-5255-4381-4 (Hardcover)
978-1-5255-4382-1 (Paperback)
978-1-5255-4383-8 (eBook)

1. JUVENILE FICTION, SOCIAL ISSUES, EMOTIONS & FEELINGS

Distributed to the trade by The Ingram Book Company

SOMETHING LOST
SOMETHING FOUND

To my Mom...for teaching me
the true meaning of life.

Ella nuzzled under her blanket. Jasper purred softly at her feet. The stars twinkled. Mr. Moon leaned into her bedroom window to say goodnight. But none of it made Ella happy. She could not sleep.

Lying in her comfy bed, she felt like a
balloon without air. Or like noodles gone
cold on a plate. Floppy. Ella felt like she
was stuck in a pile of gloomy mud.
She missed her mom so much.

At school, Margo skipped down the hall, humming to herself.
Her smile looked like a warm embrace. It invited all her friends to laugh.

Margo carried a box of tissues. She wiped her nose so often that it was red like Rudolph's. *Maybe I can catch happiness like a cold,* thought Ella.

"Please, sneeze on me," whispered Ella.

Margo's "Aa-aa-achoo" blew at Ella like a wet and chilly gust of wind.

"Bless you!" replied Ella. She threw her arms up in the air and skipped down the hall.

ACHOO!!

Ella did walk away from the sneeze with something.
But a few days later, it turned out to be just a cold.
The sniffles did not put a smile on Ella's face.

Ella stared at the ceiling from her living-room floor.
She heard her grandma talking on the phone
in the kitchen. "Well, you know how it is," Grandma
said. "Money can't buy happiness. Some of the
happiest people I know have very little money."
*That must be it, Ella thought. If I give up all my money,
maybe happiness will find me.*

Like a rocket ship, Ella flew upstairs to her room. In a single burst of energy, she tossed her piggy bank out her window. **Smash!**

"Money! Money! It's everywhere! There's so much of it," squealed a chorus of voices, belonging to the kids who lived on her street.

"It will be easy for happiness to find me at home," she whispered to herself.
Ella waited a few days. But happiness did not knock on her door.
Winter turned to spring. She waited. The only knock came from the letter carrier.

By summer, Ella thought, Maybe happiness got packaged and dropped off at my house. Maybe I just haven't noticed it yet. She checked the mailbox. Nothing. She checked underneath her doormat. Nothing.
By fall, she exclaimed, "Happiness must have lost my home address!"

Ella read a book about witches. She learned that witches made magic potions, from different ingredients, to make extraordinary things happen.

So, for Halloween, Ella wore a black dress. She rode her broomstick from house to house. She cackled loudly, before saying "Trick or treat!" at every doorstep.

Back at home, Ella got the largest pot she could find. She took it to her room and threw in all her Halloween candy. Grandma always said that chicken-noodle soup made you feel better, so Ella poured in a cup of it, and then squirted in some bubble bath. Lastly, Ella found a tuft of Jasper's fur, which she added in for good luck.

Ella stirred her potion slowly. She watched the noodles
dance with the chocolate and lollipops.
As she stirred, she sang:

"I am Ella Samantha Bean.
Happiness, happiness,
where have you been?
I am Ella Samantha Bean.
Happiness, happiness,
make yourself seen."

Ella repeated these words over and over. Soon, her eyelids felt as heavy as her school bag. Just to make sure the magic potion would really work, she climbed into the pot. Only her head and shoulders poked out.

In the morning, Ella woke up to a screechy voice. It was her older brother, Nathan. "Dad! Ella is sleeping in our good spaghetti pot!" yelled Nathan. "It smells like bubbles and chicken soup in her room! And there are sticky candy wrappers all over the floor!"

Ella could hear her dad's footsteps getting closer to her door. *Nothing about me feels extraordinary,* she thought. *Except that I'm gooey and can't see past the noodles dangling in front of my eyes.*

Her dad opened the door to her room, and smiled. "Another experiment of yours, my little bean?" Before she even opened her mouth to explain, she felt his arms around her. He squeezed her tight.

"Ella, you remind me so much of your mom. You are my sparkling little star," said her dad. "Now let's clean up this interesting soup you've made."
Her dad's loving words gave Ella an idea
I can wish upon a star for happiness!

That evening she pulled out her dad's
painting ladder and her butterfly catcher
and dragged them outside.
Then she waited until the sky was
dark with many sparkling stars.

Ella wedged the butterfly catcher between her teeth. Then she carefully climbed the ladder to the highest step, whispering, "I just need to catch one tiny star bright enough to make a wish upon it."

Ella waved the butterfly net back and forth at least five times. Suddenly, the net became a little heavier.

Ella climbed down and ran inside and
upstairs to her room. Breathing heavily
from all that star catching, she sat on her
bed and reached into the net. Her catch felt
a little prickly and rough. She opened her
fingers to discover ... a large pinecone.

Ella sighed with disappointment. She was pretty sure the pinecone wouldn't grant her wish for happiness. However, it smelled so beautiful that she put it on her bedside table. It was very late, so Ella quickly fell asleep.

Ella had a much-loved friend. She visited
her friend in the thickness of the sun's
blaze and in the numbing, unkind breath
of winter. Her friend always met her in the
same place, as if waiting for no one but Ella.
The next morning, after one of her dad's
fluffy-pancake breakfasts, Ella went
to see her dear friend.

Ella ran towards her friend and squeezed it tightly
in a long embrace. She closed her eyes and felt
the branches, the leaves, and the apples.

This apple tree was extraordinary. It sat
away from other trees on a small hill. It had
more fruit on it than any other apple
tree Ella had ever seen.

Ella leaned against the trunk
of the apple tree.
She thought about the many times her
mom had brought her there, to gather
apples for the pies they used to bake
together.

The air smelled like a jam sandwich. The leaves of the apple tree danced to the rhythm of the wind's song. In the tree's whirling dance,
Ella heard her mom's laughter.

The tree extended one of its arms towards Ella, offering her an apple. With one crunchy bite, Ella tingled with a new energy. She felt warm and cozy, just like on nights when her mom used to tuck her in. Ella's lips curled upwards. She was light and free.

Ella took a deep breath. Inside her heart, she felt a door open. And through the door... walked happiness.

the end

About the Author

Natalia Paruzel-Gibson is a recipient of the young talent award from the Turzanski Foundation. She holds a BA in History and English Literature from the University of Toronto and an MA in History. Natalia's citygirlgonecountry.blog chronicles the changes in her family's lifestyle since leaving city life for the countryside and her art installations have appeared in Toronto's Nuit Blanche. Natalia, her husband, their two children, and their wiener dog live happily in rural Halton Hills, Ontario.

CPSIA information can be obtained
at www.ICGtesting.com
Printed in the USA
LVHW072318220120
644492LV00003B/9